# Madeleine
## the Cookie
## Fairy

Special thanks to
Rachel Elliot

ORCHARD BOOKS
338 Euston Road, London NW1 3BH
Orchard Books Australia
Level 17/207 Kent Street, Sydney, NSW 2000
A Paperback Original

First published in 2013 by Orchard Books

HiT entertainment

A CIP catalogue record for this book is available
from the British Library.

ISBN 978 1 40832 500 1

1 3 5 7 9 10 8 6 4 2

Printed in Great Britain

The paper and board used in this paperback are natural recyclable
products made from wood grown in sustainable forests. The
manufacturing processes conform to the environmental regulations
of the country of origin.

Orchard Books is a division of Hachette Children's Books,
an Hachette UK company

www.hachette.co.uk

# Madeleine
## the Cookie
## Fairy

by Daisy Meadows

ORCHARD

www.rainbowmagic.co.uk

The Fairyland Palace

Candy Land

Goblins' ice cream van

Market Sta[ll]

Charlie's ice cream va[n]

Kirsty's House

Wetherbury Village

Jack Frost's
Ice Castle

Funfair

The Park

Sweet
Shop

The High St.

Jack Frost's Spell

I have a plan to cause some strife
And use those fairies to change my life.
I'm going to take their charms away
And make my dreams come true today!

I'll build a castle made of sweets,
And spoil the fairies' silly treats.
I just don't care how much they whine,
Their cakes and lollies will be mine!

# Contents

# In the Candy Land Café

The yellow walls of the *Candy Land* sweet factory were gleaming in the midday sun, and the brightly coloured flags on its roof waved in the spring breeze. In the factory café, Rachel Walker and Kirsty Tate were finishing their sandwiches and chatting to Kirsty's Aunt Harri.

"You're so lucky to work here," Rachel said. "It's my dream job!"

"You wouldn't say that if you could see all the paperwork I have to do," replied Aunt Harri with a laugh.

"Yes, but you get to taste all the new sweets," said Kirsty with a giggle. "That sounds like the best job in the world!"

Aunt Harri laughed and glanced up at the clock on the wall.

"It does mean I could organise a tour of the factory for my favourite niece and her best friend!" she said with a smile. "Have you enjoyed the tour so far?"

It was Kirsty's birthday tomorrow, and this special day at *Candy Land* was an early birthday treat. Because Rachel was staying with Kirsty over half term, she had been given a ticket too.

"It's been brilliant!" said Rachel. "The chocolate department really was amazing."

"Yes, thank you for the tickets, Aunt Harri," said Kirsty. "Today is one of the best birthday presents I've ever had!"

"It's not over yet," said Aunt Harri with a grin. "You'll be spending this afternoon with me in the cookie department. But first I've got another little treat for you. Wait here and I'll be right back."

She winked at them and headed into the café. Rachel and Kirsty looked at each other with shining eyes.

"I don't know how this day could get any better!" said Rachel. "Isn't this just perfect?"

She waved her arm around at the café tables and chairs. Everything at *Candy Land* was made to look like sweet treats, so the tables were huge cakes and the chairs were enormous cookies.

"Look," whispered Kirsty, nudging her best friend. "That boy's got a Sticky Toffo Choc. They're my favourite."

Rachel glanced at the boy, who was sitting at the next table.

"It looks lovely," she said. "I'm so glad that chocolate tastes delicious again."

The girls were in the middle of an exciting fairy adventure. Jack Frost had stolen the Sweet Fairies' magical charms, which they used to look after delicious sweets in both Fairyland and the human world. He wanted to build a giant Candy Castle with the sweets! Even worse, he was trying to spoil Treat Day in Fairyland. Usually, Queen Titania and King Oberon would give each fairy a special basket of sweet treats. But there wouldn't be any treats this year unless Kirsty and Rachel could help all seven Sweet Fairies get their magical charms back!

That morning, Jack Frost and his greedy goblins had caused a chocolate disaster at *Candy Land*. Kirsty and Rachel had helped the fairies to put everything right.

"I hope that the goblins won't cause any trouble this afternoon," said Kirsty. "But there are still three more magical objects to find, so we have to keep an eye out for them."

Jack Frost had given the objects to his goblins for safekeeping, and ordered them to bring all the sweets from the human world to his Candy Castle.

"We've already helped four of the Sweet Fairies to get their magical charms back," said Rachel. "I just hope that we can find the others before it's too late!"

# Cookie Crisis

"Aunt Harri's coming back," said Kirsty. "Let's finish talking about the goblins later."

Aunt Harri was carrying a cream bag with swirly blue writing on the side.

### Cookie Creations
*Delicious cookies made especially for you!*

17

Kirsty and Rachel looked at each other.

"Jack Frost still has Madeleine the Cookie Fairy's magical charm," said Rachel. "I get the feeling that these cookies might not be as delicious as they're supposed to be…"

"These are for you, girls," said Aunt Harri, taking two cookies from the bag. "I asked to have your names written on them, but I don't think that the person behind the counter was listening."

The girls thanked her and took the cookies. They were covered with messy splodges of icing in garish colours. Rachel and Kirsty each took a small bite and then exchanged a surprised smile.

"Wow!" said Kirsty. "This tastes scrumptious!"

"Mine too," said Rachel, taking another bite. "Delicious!"

"Glad you like  them!" said Aunt Harri with a beaming smile. "Now, it's time for us to go to the cookie department. I'm hoping that you can help me with my work."

The girls finished their cookies and Aunt Harri led them through the café.

"Look," said Rachel, pointing to the corner of the café. "That's the Cookie Creations counter."

"And there's the cookie kitchen behind it," Kirsty added.

"That's where they make the cookies and decorate them to order," said Aunt Harri.

"Mmm, I can smell the cookies baking!" said Rachel, sniffing the air in delight.

As the girls followed Aunt Harri
through the café to the cookie
department, Kirsty frowned thoughtfully.

"I don't understand how the Cookie
Creations cookies can taste so delicious
while Jack Frost has the magical cookie
charm," she whispered to Rachel.

"Perhaps Madeleine has managed to
find it in Fairyland," said Rachel.

Just then, Aunt Harri stopped outside a
door marked COOKIE
DESIGN ROOM.
She took two
white aprons
from pegs
outside the
room and
handed them
to the girls.

"Every cookie designer has to wear an apron," she said, her eyes twinkling.

When the girls opened the door, a wonderful aroma filled the air. Men and women in green aprons were hurrying to and fro, and pictures of cookies decorated the walls.

"Mmm, lovely!" said Rachel, sniffing the air in delight. "I can smell cinnamon and chocolate and roasting nuts and cookie dough!"

"I want to show you some sketches of new cookies I've designed," said Aunt Harri, leading them to a desk in the corner of the room.

She laid several sheets of paper on the desk. On each sheet was a beautiful drawing of a cookie, with tiny arrows pointing to the things that made that cookie special.

"These are Jammy Hearts," said Aunt Harri, pointing to the first design. "They're heart-shaped sandwich cookies filled with jam."

"I like the look of these," said Rachel, pointing to a cookie with a happy face made out of chocolate chips.

"Those are called Chocolate Smiles," Aunt Harri told her.

"This picture's making my mouth water," said Kirsty, looking at a design for oatmeal and raisin cookies.

"Yes, those are Oaty Surprises," said Aunt Harri. "They're my favourites too."

"If these taste half as good as the ones from Cookie Creations, they'll be great!" said Rachel.

"Thanks, girls," said Aunt Harri. "It's

good to hear that people will like them!"

Just then, the door was flung open and a man who worked in the factory hurried in, carrying a tray of cookies. He looked very upset.

"Harri, we've got a big problem," he said, holding out the tray. "All these cookies are ruined – look! I don't know what's going wrong. There's no jam in the Jammy Hearts, the Chocolate Smiles are missing the chocolate chip faces and the Oaty Surprises haven't got any raisin surprises!"

Aunt Harri frowned.

"Perhaps it's because they're so new," she said. "We must have made a mistake with the cookie machine settings."

The factory worker shook his head. "But even the traditional gingerbread cookies are turning out wrong. They've all got enormous feet and pointy ears. We've been making those for ages, so it can't be the settings."

Rachel looked at the gingerbread cookie on the tray and nudged Kirsty.

"That gingerbread man looks more like a gingerbread goblin to me," she whispered. "Kirsty, I think the goblins must be right here in the cookie department!"

# Kitchen Surprise

Aunt Harri looked worried and upset.

"Girls, do you mind waiting here while I go and check the cookie machine?" she asked. "While I'm gone, you could look through my cookie cutters and pick out the ones you like best."

She handed the girls a box that was filled with cookie cutters of every shape and size. Then she hurried off with the factory worker.

"There have been so many problems at *Candy Land* lately," Rachel and Kirsty heard her say. "I can't understand it."

The girls looked at each other. They knew why everything was going wrong!

"Jack Frost is so mean," said Kirsty.

 "Aunt Harri has been so kind to us, it's really unfair that she should have all this worry."

"If we can help all the Sweet Fairies, we'll help your Aunt Harri too," said Rachel.

"Yes," Kirsty agreed. "We just have to wait for our chance to find the next magical charm."

They started to sort through the box.
"There must be every cookie cutter
ever made here!" said Rachel with a
laugh. "Stars…butterflies…flowers…
Even gingerbread men and women!"

"Oh, look at this
one!" exclaimed
Kirsty, picking
up a castle-
shaped cookie
cutter. "It
looks just like
the king and
queen's palace in
Fairyland!"

"It's really pretty,"
said Rachel. "I wonder
if there are any more in
here."

She peered into the bottom of the box and then gave a little squeal of excitement.

"Kirsty, look!" she said. "That cookie cutter in the corner is glowing!"

"It's the shape of a fairy!" said Kirsty. "Oh Rachel, do you think it could be...?"

Rachel picked it up and the glow grew brighter. She saw a tiny puff of fairy dust around the edges of the cookie cutter, and then Madeleine the Cookie Fairy fluttered up through the middle!

"Hello, Madeleine!" said the girls in delight.

The little fairy was so pleased to see them that she turned a backwards somersault in the air. She was wearing funky purple trousers covered in colourful stars, and her cheeks were pink with excitement.

"Hello, Rachel! Hello, Kirsty!" she said, speaking very fast. "I'm so glad I've found you! The goblins are somewhere at *Candy Land* with my magical charm!"

"We think the goblins are here too," said Rachel. "Something's gone wrong with the cookie machine."

"The only cookies that haven't gone wrong are the ones we got from Cookie Creations," Kirsty added. "They were delicious."

"Oh my goodness," said Rachel, putting her hand to her mouth and opening her eyes wide. "Of course! Madeleine, I think your magical charm must be at Cookie Creations. That explains why their cookies are so scrumptious."

34

"If I don't get my charm back soon, all cookies everywhere will be ruined," said Madeleine, tucking her blonde hair behind her ears. "I have to find those goblins! Girls, will you help me?"

"Of course we will," said Kirsty and Rachel together.

"We have to go and search the Cookie Creations kitchen," Rachel added. "Do you think we've got time to go now?"

Kirsty glanced around to check that no one was looking. All the other cookie designers were hard at work. But just then, the door opened. Aunt Harri was coming back!

"Quick!" Kirsty whispered. "Hide in my apron pocket!"

Madeleine swooped into the pocket of Kirsty's apron as Aunt Harri walked over to them. She was carrying a large tray piled high with spoiled cookies.

"Have you fixed the machine?" asked Rachel.

"Not yet," said Aunt Harri with a sigh. "The engineers are working on it now. I brought the ruined cookies because even though we can't sell them in the shops, it would be a shame to waste them. They're not burnt, just a funny shape with some missing ingredients. I thought they could be used at Cookie Creations instead. We could decorate them to order and sell them at a discount."

"May we take the trays to Cookie Creations for you?" asked Kirsty at once.

Aunt Harri gave her a grateful smile. "That's really kind of you, Kirsty," she said. "It would help me a lot. These machine problems mean that I've got a lot of extra work to do."

She handed the tray to Kirsty.

"Is it all right if we have a look at the Cookie Creations kitchen while we're there?" Rachel asked.

"Of course," said
Aunt Harri. "Take
as much time as
you like, and
let the baker
know that
I said it
was okay."

The girls
hurried out of the
cookie design room and
back down the corridor towards the café.
Lunchtime had finished, so it was almost
empty. There was just one group of
people in green factory uniforms sitting
at a very messy table. They were making
so much noise that they didn't notice
Kirsty and Rachel hurry past to the
Cookie Creations counter.

The cookie baker was standing at the counter decorating cookies. His bright green apron was smeared with chocolate and jam, and there were puffs of icing sugar in the air around him. He was wearing a tall, lopsided chef's hat, which was much too big for him. All that the girls could see of his face was a long, green nose.

Rachel gasped and clutched Kirsty's arm. "He's a goblin!" she exclaimed.

# Fairies in the Factory

Kirsty gave the goblin baker the cookie tray.

"My Aunt Harri sent these," she said, pretending that she didn't know he was a goblin. "The cookie machine has gone wrong, so she would like you to sell these spoiled cookies at a discount."

The goblin curled his lip. "I don't want your horrible spoiled cookies!" he squawked.

But then he noticed the gingerbread men with big feet and pointy ears. He snatched one eagerly from the tray, grabbed some bright green icing and started to decorate it.

"Come on," whispered Rachel. "He's not watching us. If Madeleine turns us into fairies, we can search for her cookie charm while he's busy."

Kirsty and Rachel ducked down behind the display counter and Madeleine popped out of Kirsty's apron pocket. With a wave of her wand, she sent a puff of cookie-scented fairy dust over the girls. Instantly, they shrank to fairy-size and beautiful wings unfurled from their shoulders in shimmering rainbow colours.

"I love being a fairy!" said Rachel with a giggle.

She did a somersault in the air and swooped underneath Kirsty as she rose up and up.

"Me too," said Kirsty, smiling at her best friend. "But right now we have to find that cookie charm, and time's running out!"

Before they could decide where to start the search, the noisy group from the lunch table dashed up to the Cookie Creations counter.

"Hide!" whispered Madeleine. "Quick, up here!"

She led the girls up to the Cookie Creations sign above the counter, and they all perched on top of it. From there, they could see the heads of the noisy factory workers.

They were all wearing green hats and jostling against each other, trying to get close to the counter.

"Those factory workers have such enormous feet that I can see them from here," Kirsty whispered.

"I bet they're goblins too," said Rachel. "Listen to the way they're squawking!"

"More cookies!" the goblins were shouting. "More cookies NOW!"

"You've had enough," replied the harassed goblin baker. "The cookies are supposed to be for Jack Frost's Candy Castle, remember? Look what I've made to hang up on the castle walls."

He held up three cookies, which he had decorated as pictures for Jack Frost to hang on the castle walls.

"Master's pet!" sneered the other goblins, blowing loud raspberries.

"I don't care what you say," shouted the goblin baker, sticking out his tongue. "I'm going to make a goblin cookie to hang up in Jack Frost's Throne Room, and he'll be so pleased with it that he'll make me the boss of you!"

The other goblins started pulling faces at the baker.

"I'll tell him what you've been doing!" roared the baker.

"You're always sucking up to Jack Frost!" one of them complained. "Telltale!"

He put his thumb to his nose and waggled his fingers.

"Go away!" the baker shouted. "I want to finish my cookie picture!"

The other goblins stomped away, muttering to each other, and the baker gazed down at the gingerbread goblin.

"I need some chocolate chips for the face," the girls heard him say to himself. He hurried into the cookie kitchen.

"Let's follow him," said Kirsty. "He's making the delicious cookies, so I bet he has the charm."

Quietly, the girls and Madeleine fluttered after him, keeping high above his head so he didn't spot them. The sweet-smelling kitchen was warm. There were several trays of gingerbread goblins cooling on the work surface. Rachel, Kirsty and Madeleine watched the baker scurry across to the pantry. He pulled a bunch of keys from his trouser pocket.

"Girls!" said Madeleine with a squeak of excitement. "Look!"

Among the keys, they could see a small chocolate chip cookie charm. It was glowing magically.

"That's my magical charm," said Madeleine. "But how are we going to get it back?"

49

# A Green Transformation

The goblin baker used his keys to open
the pantry, and stepped inside. It was
like a small room, with just enough
space for one person to stand inside. The
walls were lined with shelves, and the
girls spotted giant jars of jam, sacks of
chocolate chips and big boxes of raisins.

"Those are all ingredients that are missing from the *Candy Land* cookies," Kirsty whispered. "That greedy goblin must have taken them all."

The baker heaved a sack of chocolate chips out of the cupboard and onto his back.

"Jack Frost will really like the gingerbread goblin," he said aloud, chuckling. "Then he'll see that I'm better than all those other stupid goblins. I know! I'll make a gingerbread Jack Frost to go with it. He'll love that!"

"I've got an idea," said Rachel. "Madeleine, can you make it seem as if the gingerbread goblins are singing? Perhaps we can distract him long enough to get the charm back."

While the baker had his back turned to lock up the cupboard, the girls flew over to the cooling trays. They each picked up a gingerbread goblin and hid behind it, while Madeleine hovered high above so she couldn't be seen.

When the goblin turned around with
the sack of chocolate
chips, Rachel
and Kirsty
started to
wiggle the
gingerbread
goblins
around, making
it look as if they
were dancing. Madeleine used her
magic to make it sound as though the
gingerbread men were singing:

*"Jack Frost takes everything sweet,*
*He's the greediest man you'll ever meet.*
*So won't you please drop that sack,*
*And give us the magical cookie charm*
*back."*

54

The goblin dropped the sack and his mouth fell open. He stared at the gingerbread goblins, jingling the key ring in his hand.

"Get ready," Kirsty whispered. "We'll just have to fly over there as fast as we can and take the charm."

But then the goblin shook his head and laughed. "I've made so many cookies that I'm imagining they can sing and dance!" he said with a cackle.

The girls would have tried again, but at that moment the door to the kitchen burst open and the noisy goblins poured into the room, yelling for more cookies. One of them grabbed the gingerbread goblin that the baker had decorated and bit its legs off. Kirsty and Rachel flew back up to join Madeleine.

"It's hopeless," said Madeleine, tears filling her eyes. "I'll never get my charm back."

"Of course you will," said Kirsty in a firm voice. "I've got a plan, and I'm pretty sure it'll work. We just have to be brave. Madeleine, I want you to disguise me and Rachel as goblins."

Madeleine's hand flew to her mouth.

"Please be careful," she said. "If they realise you're tricking them,

they might capture you and take you to the Ice Castle as prisoners."

"We have to do everything we can to get your charm back," said Rachel. "Don't worry, Madeleine. We're more than a match for those goblins!"

The girls fluttered down to the far corner of the kitchen and Madeleine waved her wand. They felt themselves growing taller, and their noses and ears became stretched and pointy. They looked at each other and grinned.

"You've gone green!" said Rachel with a giggle.

"So have you!" Kirsty replied. "And your hair has disappeared."

"I'm glad we don't have to stay like this for ever," said Rachel. "Come on, let's join the goblins. Don't forget to make your voice sound all squawky!"

# Greedy
# Guts

The girls elbowed their way past the other goblins, who were all pestering the baker.

"I've got to get on with the cookies for the Candy Castle," he shouted. "Leave me alone!"

"Just one more cookie each!" Kirsty yelled above the squeals of the other goblins. "Then we'll leave you alone!"

"Yes, just one more," said the other goblins, who always liked someone to take charge and tell them what to do. "Then we'll go away."

The baker goblin had his hands over his ears to drown out the noise.

"All right!" he hollered. "All right, one more each! Then you have to leave me alone!"

Eagerly, the goblins started to call out their orders.

"I want marzipan on mine!"

"Jelly drops!"

"Green icing!"

"I want raisins on mine," said Rachel, remembering which ingredients were locked in the pantry.

"I want jam," added Kirsty.

There was a deafening clamour as everyone called out their favourite ingredients. The baker slapped his forehead with his hand.

"Shut up, all of you!" he roared. "I can't hear myself think!"

"I'll help," said Rachel in a gruff squawk. "I'll fetch all the ingredients for you."

The baker goblin nodded eagerly. He took the keys from his pocket and threw them to Rachel.

"Got it!"
Rachel
exclaimed,
unhooking
the magical
cookie charm.

She and Kirsty
ran to the back of
the kitchen, and Madeleine swooped
down to join them.

"What are you doing?" cried the baker
in shock. He still thought that the girls
were goblins!

"I'm returning this charm to its rightful
owner," Rachel replied.

She handed the cookie charm to
Madeleine, and it glowed even more
brightly as it shrank to fairy-size.

"TRAITORS!" bawled the goblins.

"No, they're HUMANS!" said Madeleine in triumph.

She returned Rachel and Kirsty to their

normal selves, and the goblins went very quiet.

"Jack Frost is going to be furious if we go back without any cookies at all," said the baker in a small voice. "What are we going to do?"

They all hung their heads and stared

miserably at their big feet. Madeleine felt sorry for them. She waved her wand and a ribbon of fairy dust went looping around the goblins, touching each of them on the hand. Suddenly, every goblin found that he was holding a special cookie. There was even a new gingerbread goblin for the baker and a gingerbread Jack Frost for the Ice Lord.

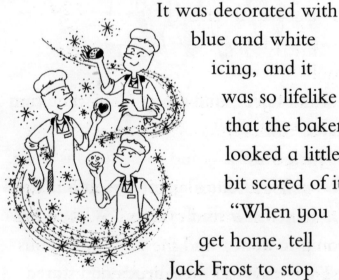

It was decorated with blue and white icing, and it was so lifelike that the baker looked a little bit scared of it! "When you get home, tell Jack Frost to stop being so greedy," said Kirsty.

"It's not fair to everyone else who likes cookies," Rachel added. "Jack Frost should learn to share!"

Madeleine gave a little twirl in the air.

"I'll take the goblins safely home," she said. "I'll make sure they don't get up to any more mischief on the way!"

"Goodbye!" said Kirsty. "Tell the other Sweet Fairies that we're here whenever they need us!"

"Goodbye, Madeleine!" called Rachel.

Madeleine waved and smiled, then her wand swooshed and she and the goblins disappeared back to Fairyland.

"Come on," said Kirsty. "Let's get back to Aunt Harri."

The girls ran all the way to the cookie department, hoping that the cookie machine would now work. When they reached the cookie design room, they found Aunt Harri coming out with a big smile on her face.

"Just in time, girls!" she said. "The engineers have fixed the cookie machine and I'm about to go and watch the first batches coming out!"

Feeling very excited, the girls followed Aunt Harri to the main factory area.

Aunt Harri pointed at a giant conveyor belt.

"Look," she said. "That's carrying the Chocolate Smiles into the oven!"

Rachel and Kirsty stood on tiptoe and saw rows of happy chocolate chip faces going into the enormous cooker.

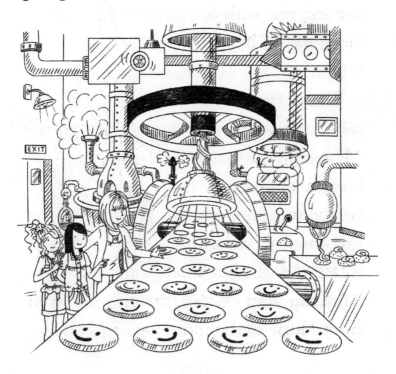

"Now come round here," said Aunt Harri.

On the other side of the machine, another conveyor belt was carrying the first batch of baked cookies out of the oven.

"Jammy Hearts and Oaty Surprises!" said Rachel, clapping her hands together in delight. "They look perfect."

"You can tell us if they taste perfect," said Aunt Harri.

She handed them each a cookie. As the girls took a bite, all the factory workers held their breath. Was all their hard work worth it?

"DELICIOUS!" said Kirsty and Rachel together.

There was a loud cheer from the factory workers, and Aunt Harri grinned happily. She picked up two boxes of cookies and handed them to the girls.

"You can take home the very first boxes from the assembly line," she said. "I hope that you've had a good time today, because I've loved showing you around."

"It's been brilliant," said Kirsty, giving her aunt a big hug. "Thank you so much, Aunt Harri. It was a fantastic birthday present!"

"Let's save the cookies for your birthday tomorrow," Rachel suggested.

"Hopefully we can eat them to celebrate finding the other magical objects," said Kirsty in a low voice. "We still have two more to find. Do you think we can do it in time for the Fairyland Treat Day?"

"Definitely," said Rachel in a confident voice. "No matter how hard he tries, Jack Frost can't get the better of us!"

**Now it's time for Kirsty and
Rachel to help...**

Layla the candyfloss Fairy

**Read on for a sneak peek...**

Kirsty Tate smiled to herself as she began
climbing the steps of the helter-skelter
with her best friend Rachel Walker.
Today, Kirsty felt like the luckiest girl
in the whole world. Not only was
it her birthday, but she was here at
Wetherbury Park funfair with Rachel,
and the sun was beaming down too.
Best of all, she and Rachel were in
the middle of another magical fairy
adventure, this time helping the seven
wonderful Sweet Fairies!

"It's a long way up," Rachel

commented from behind Kirsty as they went on climbing the steps. "We'll be able to see for miles from the top!"

"Oh yes," Kirsty agreed. Then she lowered her voice. "We might even be able to see a fairy from up there!" She crossed her fingers at the thought. Meeting another fairy would make her birthday absolutely perfect!

It was the spring holidays and so far the girls had had a very exciting couple of days. At the start of the week, Honey the Sweet Fairy had surprised them by appearing in a pile of sweets in Kirsty's bedroom. She needed the girls' help to stop Jack Frost, who was up to his naughty tricks again. This time, he'd stolen the Sweet Fairies' seven magical charms so he could build himself an enormous Candy Castle.

The Sweet Fairies worked very hard to make sure that sweets and treats in Fairyland and the human world tasted utterly scrumptious. Without the fairies' magic charms, sweet things didn't taste nice at all. Even worse, it was now the annual Treat Day in Fairyland, and the fairy king and queen wouldn't be able to give out their traditional treat baskets to the fairies, unless all seven charms were safely returned...

Read **Layla the Candyfloss Fairy** to find out what adventures are in store for Kirsty and Rachel!